W9-BFT-524

Mat

by Bobby Lynn Maslen
pictures by John R. Maslen

Scholastic Inc.

New York • Toronto • London • Auckland • Sydney • Mexico City • New Delhi • Hong Kong • Buenos Aires

Beginning sounds for Book 1:

M m — (moon

A a — 🍎 apple

T t — ⊓ table

S s — ☀ sun

Ask for Bob Books at your local bookstore, or visit www.bobbooks.com.

Thank you to Larry Sims, trumpeter for all ages, and to our editor and navigator, Shannon Penney.

No part of this publication may be reproduced, stored in a retrieval system, or transmitted in any form or by any means, electronic, mechanical, photocopying, recording, or otherwise, without written permission of the publisher. For information regarding permission, write to Scholastic Inc., Attention: Permissions Department, 557 Broadway, New York, NY 10012.

ISBN-10: 0-545-01918-4
ISBN-13: 978-0-545-01918-7

Mat: ISBN 0-545-02714-4
Sam: ISBN 0-545-02715-2
Dot: ISBN 0-545-02716-0
Mac: ISBN 0-545-02717-9

Copyright © 1976 by Bobby Lynn Maslen. All rights reserved. Published by Scholastic Inc. by arrangement with Bob Books® New Initiatives LLC. SCHOLASTIC and associated logos are trademarks and/or registered trademarks of Scholastic Inc. BOB BOOKS is a registered trademark of Bob Books Publications LLC.

6 5 4 3 2 1   7 8 9 10 11/0

Printed in China
This edition first printing, October 2007

Mat.

3

Mat sat.

Sam.

Sam sat.

Mat sat. Sam sat.

Mat sat on Sam.

Sam sat on Mat.

Mat sat. Sam sat.

The End

Sam

by Bobby Lynn Maslen
pictures by John R. Maslen

Scholastic Inc.
New York • Toronto • London • Auckland • Sydney • Mexico City • New Delhi • Hong Kong • Buenos Aires

Beginning sounds for Book 2:

C c — cat

D d — dog

Sam and Cat.

Mat and Cat.

Sam, Mat, and Cat.

Cat sat on Sam.

Mat sat on Sam.

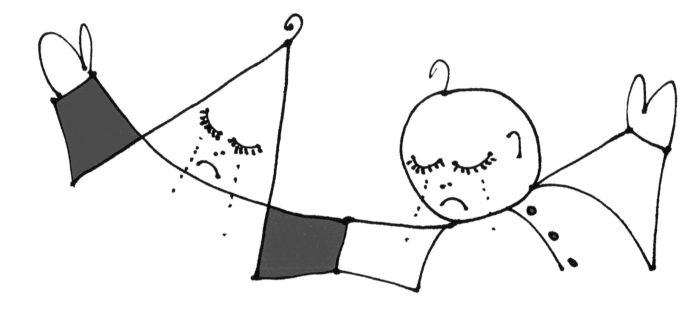

Sad Sam. Sad Mat.

Sam sat. Mat sat.

O.K., Sam. O.K., Mat. O.K.,Cat.

The End

Dot

by Bobby Lynn Maslen
pictures by John R. Maslen

Scholastic Inc.
New York • Toronto • London • Auckland • Sydney • Mexico City • New Delhi • Hong Kong • Buenos Aires

Beginning sounds for Book 3:

O o — octopus

H h — hat

G g — goat

R r — rabbit

Dot has a hat.

Dot has a cat.

The cat has a hat.

Dot has a dog. Dog has a hat.

Dog has a rag hat.

Sad dog.

Sad Dot. Sad cat.

Dog has on a rag hat.

The End

Mac

by Bobby Lynn Maslen
pictures by John R. Maslen

Scholastic Inc.
New York • Toronto • London • Auckland • Sydney • Mexico City • New Delhi • Hong Kong • Buenos Aires

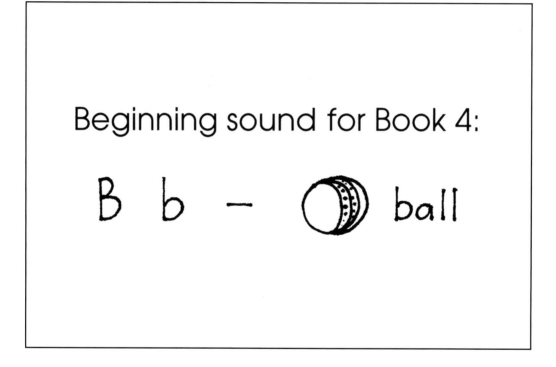

Beginning sound for Book 4:

B b — ball

Mac had a bag.

The bag had a dog.

Mac had a bag and a dog.

Mag had a rag.

Mac can tag Mag.

Mac got the rag.

Mac sat on the rag.

Mag sat on the bag.

The End

Available Bob Books®:

Set 1: Beginning Readers — With consistent new sounds added gradually, your new reader is gently introduced to all the letters of the alphabet. They can soon say, "I read the whole book!®"

Set 2: Advancing Beginners — The use of three-letter words and consistent vowel sounds in slightly longer stories build skill and confidence.

Set 3: Word Families — Consonant blends, endings and a few sight words advance reading skills while the use of word families keep reading manageable.

Set 4: Compound Words — Longer books and complex words engage young readers as proficiency advances.

Set 5: Long Vowels — Silent *e* and other vowel blends build young readers' vocabulary and aptitude.

Bob Books® Listen and Read

Listen and Read 1
Set 1: Beginning Readers 1-4 + CD

Listen and Read 2
Set 1: Beginning Readers 5-8 + CD

Listen and Read 3
Set 1: Beginning Readers 9-12 + CD

W9-BEF-699

THE

ACCELERATED
READER™

computerized reading management program

Accelerated Reader

Test # 5559

Book Level 5.3

Points 0.5

Points

AR word count: 1, 111

Christmas trees /
Henderson, Kathy.   30605
                                     394.2 Hen

A New True Book

CHRISTMAS TREES

By Kathy Henderson

CHILDRENS PRESS ®
CHICAGO

Christmas tree from Belize,
a country in Central America

PHOTO CREDITS

© WALT ANDERSON/Tom Stack & Associates—19, 31, 36

AP/Wide World Photos—29, 30

© BILLY E BARNES/TSW-Click/Chicago—16

© MATT BRADLEY/Tom Stack & Associates—40 (top right)

© BARBARA VAN CLEVE/TSW-Click/Chicago—20 (right)

© STEVEN D ELMORE/Tom Stack & Associates—42

© ROBERT FRERCK/TSW-Click/Chicago—14 (top left)

© PETER LE GRAND/TSW-Click/Chicago—15 (right)

The Granger Collection, New York—6, 7, 8, 10, 11, 12, 13 (top right and left)

Joan Kalbacken—40 (bottom left)

© T. KITCHIN/Tom Stack & Associates—21, 23 (right)

Emilie Lepthien—22, 28, 33, 34

© D.C. LOWE/Shostal/SuperStock International, Inc.—25

Norma Morrison—43 (right)

Museum of Science and Industry, Chicago, Illinois—Cover (both photos), 2, 14 (right), 40 (top left and bottom right)

Rob Outlaw Photography—13 (bottom), 14 (bottom left)

© BRIAN PARKER/Tom Stack & Associates—24 (left), 39, 44

© ROD PLANCK/Tom Stack & Associates—24 (right)

© ROD PLANCK/TSW-Click/Chicago—20 (left)

© WINSTON POTE/Shostal/SuperStock International, Inc.—4, 15 (left)

MILLARD SHARP/TSW-Click/Chicago—23 (left)

WILLIAM THOMPSON/Shostal/SuperStock International, Inc.—43 (left)

© CARY WOLINSKI/TSW-Click/Chicago—27

Cover—Left: Swedish Christmas tree
        Right: Korean Christmas tree

Library of Congress Cataloging-in-Publication Data

Henderson, Kathy.
   Christmas trees.
   Includes index.
   Summary: Background lore on Christmas trees and a discussion of how they are grown for decorating our homes at Christmas.
   1. Christmas trees—Juvenile literature.
[1. Christmas trees]   I.   Title.
GT4989.H46   1989   394.2'68282   89-859
ISBN 0-516-01162-6

Copyright © 1989 by Childrens Press®, Inc.
All rights reserved. Published simultaneously in Canada.
Printed in the United States of America.
   2 3 4 5 6 7 8 9 10 R 98 97 96 95 94 93

TABLE OF CONTENTS

FOREVER GREENS

Since earliest times,
people have believed that
plants and trees that
stayed green all year were
special. They didn't lose
leaves or die in autumn
like many other plants
did. People used them as
symbols of life and eternity
in many celebrations.

Ancient Egyptians
brought green palm
branches into their homes

Saturnus

Woodcut made in 1482 showing *Saturn*, the Roman god of seedtime.

during the gray days of winter.

Each December, Romans celebrated *Saturnalia* to honor Saturn, the Roman god of seedtime and plenty. Buildings were decorated with evergreens

Roman villa

such as laurel and ivy to
welcome the sun's return
as the days started getting
longer. Soon it would be
time to plant the spring
crops.

A druid gathers
evergreens. According to
ancient stories, druids
were also wizards.

In ancient times, the
druids of England also
used evergreens, especially
trees, during winter as a
symbol of the coming of
spring.

THE FIRST CHRISTMAS TREE

As Christianity spread, people who loved their old folk customs began to adapt them by giving them new Christian meanings. There are many legends that tell how Christians first used evergreens to celebrate the Christmas season.

Saint Boniface was an English missionary who

Wood engraving of
Saint Boniface
declaring
Pepin the Short,
king of the Franks

brought Christianity to
Germany around A.D. 720.
Many believe he was the
first person to use an
evergreen tree as a
special symbol of Christ.
Another man who lived

Martin Luther and his family celebrate Christmas Eve at Wittenberg in 1536.

in Germany many years later is given credit for bringing the first evergreen tree into his home and decorating it during the Christmas season. His name was Martin Luther.

Since the 1600s the Christmas tree has played an important part in Christmas celebrations. In the 1800s Santa Claus (above) was added to many traditional celebrations.

Today people of many
faiths around the world
still use evergreen plants
and trees to celebrate the
winter holidays. Whether

Many people like to cut down their own Christmas trees.

they are celebrating the birth of Christ or just the joy of the season, the favorite evergreen of all is the Christmas tree.

GROWING CHRISTMAS TREES

Each year over 30 million Christmas trees are sold throughout the United States. Many more are sold in Canada and other countries around the world.

Do you know where all these trees come from? Most come from farms that grow crops of Christmas trees just as other farmers grow crops of corn and vegetables.

Unlike most farm crops, Christmas trees cannot be planted and harvested in the same year. They can take anywhere from five to sixteen years to reach the right size. How long it takes depends on what type of evergreen tree it is and how big the buyers want their Christmas tree to be.

Opposite page: Young Douglas firs on a tree farm in Oregon

Baby Christmas trees are started in nurseries. Fertilized seeds are collected from the cones of the best and hardiest trees. The Christmas trees must grow evenly and hold their needles well after being cut. The seeds are

Blue spruce cone (below) and white pine cone (right)

Seedlings are grown in nurseries.

planted in long beds of
specially prepared soil,
where they will be
protected and cared for.

The seedlings grow very
slowly. It may be two to
five years before a

Six-year-old Douglas fir

seedling is strong enough
to be sold to a Christmas-
tree farm. Some five-year-
old seedlings are only
as long as your finger.
And some two-year-old
ones are hardly bigger
than a penny!

A farmer may have

Western white spruce seedling (left) and long-leafed pine seedling (right)

several varieties and ages
of Christmas trees growing
in different fields around
the farm. Each area of the
country has a type of tree
that grows best.

In the Pacific Northwest,

Dew-covered blue spruce branch (above) and
a black spruce (right) growing amid bog laurel

Midwest, and northern
Atlantic states, where most
Christmas trees are grown,
Douglas fir, balsam, and
spruce are favorites.
Virginia pine grows best in
southern states like
Louisiana and Mississippi.
Even in parts of California
where the ground is not

Christmas tree farm in Oregon. Mount Hood is in the background.

very good for growing any
crop, Christmas-tree
farmers can grow a hardy
evergreen called the
Monterey pine.

Altogether, more than
500,000 acres of land in
the United States are used
for growing Christmas trees.

SHEARING
AND SHAPING

Left to grow wild, few evergreen trees would develop the traditional cone shape and thick, bushy branches that most buyers want. So Christmas-tree farmers help things along by shearing and shaping each growing tree. The trees are sheared from one to three times during late spring through early fall each year.

Farmers use a variety of

Workers move through a Christmas tree forest.

tools. On small farms, all
of the work may be done
by hand with large knives.
It takes a worker with a
strong arm but a light
touch to shape a tree
just right. Other workers

Trees marked with colored ties will be pruned.

prefer special pruning shears that look somewhat like the pliers that a carpenter uses. The shears are sharpened to cut cleanly through a tough branch.

This machine
wraps the trees
for shipping.

On large farms, specially
designed machines are
used to do everything from
setting new seedlings in
the ground to shaking
dead needles from a tree
before it is cut. Shearing
machines might run on
hydraulic power from a
tractor. Hand-held

This horizontal saw is used to cut trees in Indiana, Pennsylvania.

machines have rotary blades similar to chain saws or even roadside grass mowers.

HARVESTING

The harvest season is the busiest time of year on a Christmas-tree farm. It may begin as much as three months before the holiday.

In late fall, tree farmers go through their fields and mark trees for cutting, carefully selecting a variety of types and sizes. Usually only part of a field is cut each year. It may take three to five years before all the trees in one field are cut. Care must

Scotch pine, white pine, and Douglas fir trees are grown on this farm.

be taken to leave enough
good trees for the next
year's harvest.

After tagging, the trees

are cut by hand or by special machines. In some areas, customers can come directly to the farm and pick the tree they want and cut it themselves.

Trucks, wagons, and even helicopters are used to haul the cut trees to collection yards. Then the trees are wrapped, stacked, and loaded onto trucks and railroad cars. Some trees even travel by ship to other countries.

IMPROVING
THE ENVIRONMENT

Unlike some other types of tree harvesting done in forests, Christmas-tree growing and harvesting does not damage the environment. In fact, with good management, a Christmas-tree farm actually helps the environment.

It beautifies the landscape, particularly in areas where other crops won't grow. The trees help keep the soil from eroding. Christmas trees also act like little air conditioners, purifying the air. One acre of trees can put out enough fresh oxygen to

Christmas tree farms and natural forestlands (above)
are important to our environment.

supply eighteen people.
Christmas trees also
provide cover for many
birds and other wildlife.

39

Tree from Switzerland (above left), tree from San Antonio, New Mexico (above right) with chili pepper lights, tree from Mexico (below right), tree with Scandinavian decorations (below left)

SHARING THE CHRISTMAS TREE SPIRIT

For a long time decorating the Christmas tree has been a favorite winter holiday tradition of people in Europe and America. Each country, and even each ethnic group, has its own collection of special decorations and unique ways of celebrating.

However, one tradition
seems best to symbolize
the holiday season and the
joy of giving. It comes
when the regular holidays
are over.

After the lights and
fancy decorations and

tinsel are put away, some
people leave on the
strings of popcorn and
cranberries. They add little
tubs of suet and birdseed.
Then they set their
Christmas trees outside so
the winter birds and small
animals can enjoy their
own special Christmas tree
that is forever green.

WORDS YOU SHOULD KNOW

druid(DROO • id) — a priest of the ancient religion of Ireland, France, and England

environment(en • VYE • run • mint) — all the things that surround a person, plant, or animal, such as the air, soil, or city streets

eroding(ih • ROH • ding) — washing or blowing away

eternity(ih • TER • nih • tee) — time without end; all time forever

ethnic group(ETH • nik GROOP) — people who have the same language and customs, usually people from the same country or area

fertilized(FER • tih • lyzed) — having the parent male and female sex cells joined; ready to grow

hardy(HAR • dee) — strong and healthy; able to withstand harsh conditions

hydraulic(hi • DRAW • lik) — operated by the force of a moving liquid

legend(LEH • jind) — a story about people or events in the past

purify(PYOO • rih • fy) — to make clean; to remove pollution

rotary(ROH • tuh • ree) — going around and around

Saturnalia(sat • er • NAHL • ya) — the Roman festival of midwinter

shearing(SHEER • ing) — cutting or clipping to make shorter or to shape something

suet(SOO • it) — hard animal fat that is used in cooking and to feed birds in winter

symbol(SIM • bul) — an object that stands for another object or for an idea

unique(yoo • NEEK) — the only one of its kind

INDEX

About the Author

Kathy Henderson is Executive Director of the National Association for Young Writers, vice president of the NAYW Board of Trustees, and Michigan Adviser for the Society of Children's Book Writers. She works closely with children, teachers, and librarians through young author conferences and workshops, and is a frequent guest speaker in schools. An experienced freelance writer with hundreds of newspaper and magazine articles to her credit, she is also the author of the Market Guide for Young Writers. Mrs. Henderson lives on a 400-acre dairy farm in Michigan with her husband Keith, and two teenage children.